Space Exploration
Strange New Worlds

Other Titles from
Space Cowboy Books

Books:

Dreaming of Autonomous Vehicles – Jaroslav Olša, Jr.

The Future is Brief – Jean-Paul L. Garnier

Wave IX – Various Authors

The Martians – Emilie Procházková

Mexicans on the Moon – Pedro Iniguez

Another Time: Time Travel Stories 1942–1960

Complete Poems 1965–2020 – Michael Butterworth

Simultaneous Times Vol. 3 – Various Authors

Simultaneous Times Vol. 2.5 – Various Authors

Simultaneous Times Vol. 2 – Various Authors

Simultaneous Times Vol. 1 – Various Authors

Garbage In, Gospel Out – Jean-Paul L. Garnier

Betelgeuse Dimming – Jean-Paul L. Garnier

Future Anthropology – Jean-Paul L. Garnier

Chapbooks:

The Reducing Flame – Richard Magahiz

Micropoetry for Microplanets – Brian U. Garrison

Shelf Life – F. J. Bergmann

Mars Maundering – Denise Dumars

The Telepathy Machine – Jean-Paul L. Garnier

Time's Arrow – Jean-Paul L. Garnier

Utopian Problems – Jean-Paul L. Garnier

www.spacecowboybooks.com

Space Exploration
Strange New Worlds

John C. Mannone

ISBN: 979-8-9896308-9-9

Edited by Jean-Paul L. Garnier

First Edition | 2025

Space Cowboy Books

61871 29 Palms Hwy.

Joshua Tree, CA 92252

www.spacecowboybooks.com

Table of Contents

Acknowledgments

I wish to thank the following venues—their publishers and editors—in which some of the poems had first appeared:

Abyss & Apex [Ark II]

Altered Reality Magazine [Martian Summer; In three point five billion years; A Mere Million Miles From Earth (2024 Rhysling Award nominee); Star Map; Waterworld]

Beyond Strange Stars (TL;DR Press) [Gliese 581g]

Drabble Harvest 14: ExtraTerrestrial Reincarnation [Voyager III]

Eldritch & Ether Anthology (Black Hare Press) [An Ominous Sun]

Mystic Nebula [Beyond the Stars]

Red Fez [Eulogy for a Voyager]

Songs of Eretz Poetry Review [Mother Nature's on the Run; Breathe]

*Star*Line* 41.5 [Mission Phoenix 3]

Sublimation: a Magazine of Speculative Poetry and Art [On Kepler 452b]

Swiss American Historical Society Review 42 (1), 2, 2006 ["A Propensity for Genius: That Something Special About Fritz Zwicky (1898-1974)," John Charles Mannone [Through the Keyhole]

Trapezium [Orion Astronomy Newsletter, March 2012] and
The Cleveland Banner [excerpts in September 4, 2005] [Almanac of Planets]

Introduction

Space Exploration: Strange New Worlds is a chapbook collection that poetizes literary journalism, science, science fiction, and science fantasy. The ventures into outer space are born out of mankind's natural curiosity and perhaps also as a means of the anticipated survival of our species, but the exploration is tempered with a longing for home. At times, there is a nod to the human condition, ecological responsibility, and to the sacred beyond science. This collection strives to make literary poetry and genre poetry an inseparable fusion.

Dedication

This collection is dedicated to all of us who yearn to explore the unknown, but most especially to Roy W. Morrow (September 28, 1942 – April 4, 2019), a chemist, an amateur astronomer, and most importantly, a friend to many, who left this world much too soon.

Running Free

I feel the thrust of youth
bolt through corral gates
made of steel—

catapult like a bronco
into the Olympian void.

For a moment, I am Pegasus
dragging reins, mane stiffened
in the wind, heart pounding

like unthrottled engines
throbbing anapestic beats.

My eyes fix upon the stars
search for other steeds
that also fled for freedom—

these winged horses of Vikings,
Voyagers sailing endless seas

gallop the black plains
among sagebrush stars, ranging
from one unknown to another

and ride into a million sunsets
kicking up stardust on the trail.

Almanac of Planets

Sol

Guardian of the planets, our sun casts its light
created in its nuclear cauldron, bathes the circling
orbs glinting as pearls against a velvet black.

Mercury

Red-hot garnet near the Sun's warping
of space and time, quickly slips around
the seething glare; its molten face, staring.

Venus

Goddess in a slow dance, spins contrary
to the other orbs. Her day is in lock step
with her year.

Her garden paradise that's imagined
beneath the canopy of clouds, hides a hell
of hot choking gas thick with sulfuric
and bone-washing nitric acid rains.

Mars

Escape to shades of bright plum dissolving
through the thin cold veil draping desolation.

Windstorms scour the rusty landscape eerie
with dust-haunting sunsets in ghostly blue.

Solar winds, too, pummel the planet—a sea
of charge crashes its shores, but there is no
sea-break, no magnetic shield to fend off
the unfriendly surf that drowns
                                    any chance
                                    to flourish life

Asteroids
Do they speak of life? Some say they might
be fragments of an ancient planet crushed
by cosmic collisions—a belt of tumbling debris,
jagged chunks buckling under Newton's nudges.

Some of those shattered rocks become rogue
rockets packed with our possible extinction

Jupiter
A king with banded crown of reds and browns
blending with the cream-colored clouds—
windswept like the swirls in Arizona sandstone.

It protects us with a scepter of gravity, tidal forces
tear apart the doomsday rocks that venture too close
plunging their pieces into the mote of poison gas.
Remnant comet dust whisks into solar wind

Saturn
Painted toxic topaz, sulfur-tinged so light,
it would float across a river of stars
if the Milky Way were a river.

Spinning forces squash this pale yellow giant
with a thousand rings of rock and ice
corralled by shepherd moons

Uranus
Its spinning axis tips beyond a casual obliquity
and its magnetic axis rolls along the orbit path.

Shades of jade soften with the blue gray
yet the tranquil calm of color obfuscates
a tempest, a supersonic fury of marsh gas winds
over cryogenic plains.

Neptune
Sun's most distant native son for 20 years
out of its 248-year orbit, but mostly slips
its orbit inside Pluto's.

The planet is mostly frozen and forgotten.
            What kind of ocean does it rule?
Its gray eye, fixed on swirling seas that churn
the mighty storms with colossal waves
that wisp and curl as if an eyelid lash,
but all we see is the small green smudge
of its iris

    Pluto
The planet that is not a planet.
It's not a gas giant nor one of the in crowd
of the rocky inner planets.

Perhaps it's a refugee from the Oort cloud,
captured and destined to its eccentric orbits
much different from all the rest, perhaps
it's just a burned-out comet made of dirty ice
and laced with hydrocarbon tars.

    Earth
Best of all the havens in the heavens, she
suspends on nothing; she is fragile, yet fertile,
terrestrial, aqueous, ethereal; an atmosphere
of breath spoken into existence and perfectly
placed, third planet from the Sun.

**Before You Consider Moving, Stop
& Stare in Awe at the Northern Lights**

> *The Geophysical Institute has forecast a major solar storm
> [Kp index 6] expected to light up the skies in 17 states with the
> Northern Lights on July 13, 2023*
> —New York Post by Associated Press

Auroras are beautiful
all because the sun gets riled up
from twisted magnetic fields

that snap like rubber bands
releasing megatons of energy
streaming our way

at a sizzling million miles per hour.
Earth's own magnetic fields divert
the solar wind—like a rock

in the middle of a stream
pushing the water away and around—
lest the planet's air ablates away.

Nevertheless, some hot electrons
slip through and gyrate about the field
lines in an ever-decreasing radius.

Point your antenna-ear
at the magnetosphere above the sky
and hear the energetic electrons

whistle in a descending cascade
of pitch. But there's no screaming
when they crash into the thinning

gas above the poles and arctic rims
where the atmosphere explodes
into shimmering curtains of excited

molecules of nitrogen and oxygen
whose waves of color veil
the heavens—ruby and emerald,

amethyst and sapphire—
their dance of colors "awakens"
the God of creation just in time

to hear us sing in chorus
with the angels, a melodic ode
of praise, a song of thanks.

Just days before the Northern Lights, I drove a U-Haul truck while moving from KY back to TN with a mural about space weather [#89 in the Venture Across America series], which I used as a prompt for an Ekphrastic Workshop that I facilitate; I wondered what it would be like to move to another solar system.

The Kp Index [ranging from 0 to 9] is derived from the German, *Planetarische Kennziffer*, meaning Planetary Index, which is a measure of geomagnetic activity in Earth's atmosphere.

Beyond the Stars

> *Standing alone in the silent hills,*
> *hands folded on the controls*
> *of a great radio telescope, I pray*
> *to hear what the heavens declare.*

My ear, lifted in reticulations of steel,
presses its aluminum timpani
to her bosom, the soft hiss
of her breath like a kiss in the night.

I touch her face, every smooth
piece of sky, every wrinkle
of starlight. I cannot see with my eyes
but feel the Braille of her, with the tips

of my fingers telescoping the dark,
read her contours with oscilloscopes—
every jot and tittle
that fabrics the heavens.

I do not know how to hear
her susurrations, but I cup my ear,
point the antenna-stethoscope
towards her heart. For a moment,

I understood why Robert Frost
would choose something like a star,
but I plead beyond the stars.

I feel her pulse,
sense the cosmic echoes there,
listening with my own heart.
… I hear the small still whispers.

Nights Are Forever Without You
> *After England Dan and John Ford Coley*

It is past the equinox
and the days are shorter.

But no matter the season,
the days are long and sleep
absent; good dreams, short.

Still, the days are very long
without you and empty
        nights, longer yet.

The last time I saw you
moonlight fell like rain

and your eyes glistened
a galaxy of tears, and stars
        eclipsed in mine.

But here on the moon
it is lonelier yet, assuaged
for a moment at Earthrise.

Even this far, my heart
is tidally locked to yours—
        I feel the pull.

Contemplating Sand Traps

I stare into the distance * wonder if what is par for the course * will give me hints to make a good game plan * I reach for the nine driver * swing, pivot, and slice the ball * launching ten degrees above the short-cut grass * with enough backspin to lift it up way beyond * what mere gravity would allow * dimples on the ball reducing drag * But sand traps lurk * in the open spaces, even in stark daylight, the sun casting shadows.

I stare into the distance * to a faint plum red glow on the horizon * Mars' kicked-up dust scattering rust-colored light * over an overgrown land of sand traps and dead volcanoes that once might have given life to such a distant world. Water is needed * not for those pesky water hazards near the green * but for the incubation of life.

Some say that its oceans were delivered, like ours were, by asteroids * Not water *per se* but by minerals rich in elements of hydrogen and oxygen * Beautiful heat from thousands of super-volcanic eruptions melted the rocks releasing those elements * that combined to make the seas * Some say that there was once ten times the volume of our oceans trapped inside Earth's mantle * Where did all that water go?

And I pray:

> O Oceans, who once had flowed on Mars / What mysteries did you birth? / I see no coral, no carbonate rock to speak of life / Did Olympus Mons, your monstrous volcano, one hundred times larger than Hawaii's Mauna Loa / make bone-dissolving acid rain — sulfuric, hydrochloric, phosphoric— that erased any hint of life from us?

> Where did your three-billion-year-old oceans go? / The irony of asteroids that bringeth, then taketh away / that awaken calderas and tsunamis / to reshape the land / before the dying magma-made magnetic fields yielded to the pummeling of solar winds / that buffeted and

ablated the atmosphere / until there was nothing left but
a thin, cold veil.

But we on Earth have an atmosphere * we have molten internals to dynamo our magnetics * that protect against the disappearance of our vital air * How fortunate * Mars and Venus in conjunction once every two or three years * when I can think of war and love in the same breath, in the same swing of the four club, in the differences between planets, between people. If "men are from Mars, and women are from Venus," then we're in trouble from the get-go.

I stare into the distance * sun's fire thick with memories just ducking below the horizon * Memories of an atmosphere that once trapped a little heat * and how that was good for Mars * because the light of our yellow star is too weak there, and cold.

But what about Venus, which is much closer to the sun, boasting its diamond light? I realize why the evening star is so bright * A high albedo * because the sun reflects right off the tops of thick carbon dioxide clouds * while below, a runaway greenhouse effect traps 900-degree heat on the surface of the planet.

I don't imagine playing golf there either.

The Weatherman

It's a cool day and a local wind
is kicking up a Georgia-red dust.

Soon the sun will bloat.
There are signs in the thinning air.

Weather on the face of the sun
tempestuous, solar wind blowing

a million miles per hour after
a coronal mass ejection

from a monster sunspot
disentangling its magnetic fields

snapping back like rubber bands
to release all its energy. The sting.

Ever since I took this position
as weatherman, though a short-term

assignment, the money and promises
good, yet lonely. And I deeply miss

the sunsets by the ocean—
a refreshing breeze on our faces,

you in my arms, and a kiss
of Earth in the cup
             of my hands.

Martian Summer

It's a hot summer day, seventy degrees at the equator
but the carbon dioxide atmosphere, a very thin thermal
blanket, is not thick enough to prevent the plummet
to one hundred degrees below at night. Frost forms
on the rust-red rocks, sublimes at dawn, leaves puddles
of water for my wife and I to poach. We feel like lichens
in an arid arctic tundra. We would not survive the trek
to the polar caps to retrieve more water below dry ice
sheets, which disappear this time of year. Some say
the planet is emerging from an ice age, glaciers forming
just north of us. We must hurry, dust storms will soon
be here. We long to see our home—lost in Sun's glare.

In our dome, we embrace, make love, marvel at blue
sunsets in exceeding cold, still, there's a sense of warmth,
a hazy hint of Earth's Rayleigh scattered sky.

An Ominous Sun

Slate blue, the clouds shred in a wind shear wind
streaking by at seventy miles per hour, but everything
is relative. The windshield blasted by reddish pulver—
Georgia red, and the grit of silica sand. Feels global
                    like those dust storms on Mars
that I've studied. A bit of platinum yellow jaundices sky.
The last time we saw that, the ominous sun flared
right at us. Don't worry, Honey, the grid's protected,
we won't be plunged into darkness. We have emergency
                    backup power.
There's a rainbow encoded in all the angst, the pending
darkness. Why is the sun so angry? Its red pupil, shaped
persimmon, paling amarillo, enshrouded with a purpling
fear inked with indigo—fury's ego in the chaos—the faded
                    blue sky turning malachite green
from its envy of the coming night. In a strange way,
this reminds me of the sunsets back home—before
all the turmoil, and riots, all the killing by gangs and
by the virus—back home so far away, my birthplace,
                    my planet, my Earth.

In three point five billion years

Our Sol will begin to bloat
Planets swallowed in red glare
The Kuiper Belt soon loosened

Frozen graves will resurrect
A million comets will rain
Down on us like fireworks

We'll be long gone beforehand
Before Sun's funeral veil
Draws its nebulosity

Don't Wait Too Long to Leave for Another Star

We will continue with increasing awe
when the sun's face gets blotted with
even more sunspots that betray

the soon-to-snap magnetic loops
dripping with plasma that thunders
their cosmic spell on planet Earth

but when our yellow dwarf sun
has grown, consuming all its fuel
stored at its very core by fusion—

that simple and ubiquitous gas, hydrogen
that populates the entire universe,
there will be the inevitable victor, gravity,

in the celestial tug-of-war. The star's fire
and pressure is what holds off the crush
for now. Our sun is stubborn,

it will not yield. Instead the heat
of gravity's squeeze will ignite the leftovers
from all that hydrogen fusion, and helium

will become the sun's new meal.
With no squeaky Donald Duck voice
but rather the locomotive roar

of a Superman sun bloating in fierce
retaliation making gravity back off
(at least for a little while longer).

Our sun will then boast when
it has grown from dwarf to yellow giant
(on its way to becoming a red one

when Mercury, Venus, Earth, and Mars
will be consumed by the intumesced sun).
Other stars like ours have already testified

to the same fate. But do not cry or let your
heart be troubled, our distant relative suns
have given us life and the very oxygen
                                    we breathe.

If we stay, we will die so that others may live
when our sun will be cast into dimness
yet will remain the hot ember of a white dwarf.

Mission Phoenix 3

Scaffolding braces against yesterday,
a patch of metal bones from salvage,
dull gray in the dimming sun. Sleek,
the rocket leans into steel grapples,
stands waiting for the last countdown
… four, three, two, one, current surge,
Ignition … thrusters roar blasting denial
of gravity's hold. Motion. The squeal
of metal—cage breaking free the bird,
now resurrected soaring high through
rain-thickened sky, its pearly light gone
before punching into vapid loneliness
of outer space. Just the eight of us, last
survivors, en route to Saturn's Enceladus.

Eulogy for a Voyager

> *On August 25, 2013, spacecraft Voyager 1 left our solar
> system, crossing the heliopause into interstellar space*

O wanderer, lonely messenger
free from hold of gravity,
free to sift the stardust between stars,
to touch the face of God,

your nuclear heart pulses, keeps you
alive and warm enough to call me
home, billions of miles away … too
far, solar wind to your back, voice

fading after crossing turbulence.
In darkness, you search for answers,
but only find more questions.
The whole host of heaven smiles.

And I too stand on the precipice
of the universe, to catch that faint
glint, the final cry lost in static hiss
—that silvery light-thread of my soul.

Into shards of memory, we look back,
see only a smattering of planets
and our home, that bone white speck
in the glare of a dimming sun.

Through the Keyhole

     The Hubble Space Telescope

it slews through the vacuum of darkness—
no air to hear it whir. A lone
sentinel searching for the light of stars.

Its pupil, wide as a giant owl's
five hundred times bigger straining light
for a million seconds. Stares down
the dark like a nocturnal bird on the prowl

for mice colliding in the dark field
or where tadpoles arc their escape,
their tails forming wakes in a pond of galaxies.

A deep field filled with sparkles—
spirals, fuzzy ovals—iridescent eyes
pink, vermillion, like shrimp's eyes
on night corals.

Each speck, a starburst shrouded
with a hundred billion stars— seething
cauldrons with the magic of alchemy
breathing atoms to the edge of creation:

     my atoms of stardust
     wisping so far back
     in time
          you can almost hear
          His whisper, an echo
          in the cosmic dust.

The keyhole is a very small piece of the heavens in the Big Dipper that before 1995 was believed to contain no stars. Instead, what was discovered, was a universe of 100 billion galaxies, each with a hundred billion stars. The exposure was called the Hubble Deep Field (HDF, 1995) and the refined Hubble Ultradeep Field (HUDF, 2003/2004). Having advanced even more, the Hubble Extreme Deep Field (XDF, 2012) could see into the infrared as well and doubled the exposure revealing galaxies formed 13.2 billion years ago (https://www.planetary.org/space-images/20121008_xdf_image). The James Webb Space Telescope (2022) has revealed an incredible amount of detail. Two of the impressive images called The Tadpole Galaxy (https://science.nasa.gov/asset/hubble/the-tadpole-galaxy-distorted-victim-of-cosmic-collision/) and The Mice, catch the collision of galaxies (https://science.nasa.gov/image-detail/idl-tiff-file-40/).

What Is Dark Matter?

Sanguine, blood-swollen suns,
massive ones, have left their legacies

in the bones of my ancestors
and in mine too, the stardust

and the gold that trace the black hole
        of my own heavy heart.

Eighty percent of all the mass
in the universe is invisible,

yet the motions of stars and galxies
tells how much is there, whether

they be dim brown dwarfs, white
ones, neutron stars, something

supermassive or perhaps exotic
holding the universe together
                like love.

                ~~~

What is love—this dark matter
of the heart?

Martin Luther King, Jr.
said, *Love is the only force capable of transforming
        an enemy into a friend.*

And Mahatma Ghandi said, *When the power
of love overcomes the love of power
        the world will know peace.*
                ~~~

I understand the ubiquitous, yet elusive dark
matter much better than the astrophysics
          of love.

Mother Nature's on the Run

—After Neil Young's 'After the Gold Rush'

I never thought the Sun,
an orb of gold
light
        could flare
all the way through cold
space ninety-three million miles
        and singe
our souls in the time of apocalypse.

We were too busy
                making our own fire
bombs, blasting everything we knew.
        This good earth, stained with blood.
It must have been when the rocks cried
    that the Moon yelled
            at the Sun.
It must have been soon after that—
the gold Sun rushed its fire-light.

Only a few of us escaped
                the tsunami
fireballing at a million miles an hour,
our silver spaceships glinting
        in the hot star
light.

Mother Nature's on the run, we're flying
to a new home in the stars
    but nothing's new, no nothing's new
under any sun.

A Mere Million Miles From Earth

> The James Webb Space Telescope
> successfully manages orbital insertion into
> the Earth-Sun Lagrange Point, L2, at 2:05
> pm EST on January 24, 2022.
>
> > Sensitive instruments will be able
> > to obtain infrared images of giant
> > planets.
> > —NASA/Science: Other Worlds

Just this week, a peek through a window
into the past, into our early universe:
the image of a very young galaxy, thirteen
point five billion years ago, at the edge
of creation. Echoes

from the Big Bang pervade the night sky
—the cosmic background radiation—
high energy light stretched into invisibility,
into the microwave after having traveled
at the speed of light for 13.8 billion years.
If we could see that "color," the night sky
would blaze with light, and the twinkling
of a hundred billion galaxies.

What habitable worlds will it find? Certainly
ones with oceans. Hot jupiters. Their orbits,
close-in to their dim red suns, tidally locked
showing only one face to the hot light,
the other to the cold dark. On the surface

solar radiation would penetrate astronaut
flesh, damage DNA: free radicals running
rampant, mutations inevitable, if not
complete cell death.

Fortunately, there'll be no micrometeors
to puncture suits there, only in outerspace
is where their blood would boil in the perfect
vacuum then sublime to frozen remains
in just three degrees above absolute zero.

But on that giant planet, in its pole-to-pole
swath a thousand miles wide, a temperate
zone reminiscent of our own crescent moon's
shadow-edge

       that might be imagined with a colony
       of survivors before the Earth would suffer
       a cataclysmic collision, or other extinction
       level event—even by our own hand.
                     What a shame
       we aren't better stewards of our own
       ecology, our environment. At this pace,
       more than our dreams will runaway.

There, in the intertidal zone, we'd build,
with cleverly adapted terrestrial tools,
cozy geodesic domes with ultraviolet
shields, then gaze at the twilight sky
tagged with many moons; marvel
at the stars we could see. We'll strain
to find the tiny yellow sun's system
from where we came, and dream

of cool April showers, while snuggled
on a wooden swing for two, our feet
slapping the creaking floor boards
as if in a dance under a thin tin roof
with a pelting rain swishing rhythm, its
percussive music drifting to the yellow
crocuses bursting through the rich soil
at garden's edge; hummingbird feeders
spilling sweet sugarwater while swaying

in the breeze filled with petrichor;
    and the robbins singing
    just before the rain.

A Red Plague

There is no escape. Every star will die.
The ones that are massive, catastrophically
explode in supernovas [sterilizing everything
                    within 176 trillion miles].

And the smallest ones, the red dwarfs,
which overrun the universe, will suffer
a much slower death, turn blue perhaps
(none have died yet in the past 14 billion
years). However, they are no safe havens.

Small and dim, a "habitable place"
might be too close to the red dwarf,
so close that it would be locked

in the same way the moon is forced
to keep its same face to Earth:
one face will always stare at the small
but fiery sun, while the dark face will
be doomed to the cold.

What will we become to survive
those two faces of hell? A liminal space
between light and darkness, a twilight

shadowland—the terminus might be
temperate and windy but even there
we could only stay for a short while
before all the malevolent UV light
would sunburn us to death.

Not much natural protection. Yet fantastic
aurora lights might shimmer over the horizon
before we would have to retreat, submerge,

breathe with our modified lung-

gills, and fishtail to safer depths—pray
the flexing of the planet's crust didn't
alter the morphology of our home
and that the tidal pools would still be there

and deep enough for us to live.

Deep Impressions

Every time I see a crater, I think of extinction
and of massive meteor bombardments like
the kind that killed *Tyrannosaurus rex* when
a mountain-sized rock flew into Earth at thirty
thousand miles per hour. An impact that big
here might crack this planet to pieces.

Bring the rover closer to the rim, train
your instruments on the glistening white remnants
of water ice at the base of the crater. But stay clear
of the inky blackness. Move quickly, the storm
is coming, clouds are gathering in the blueberry
sky—that ominous dark, blue gray, just like before.

Next time, what will be left if a larger mountain
smashes into us? Vaporization will be instantaneous
on impact, tsunami shockwaves will melt this planet,
recrystallize it, leaving a crown-shaped ring full of gems
and sintered bones and the heavy falling of gray snow
in winter's nuclear sunlight.

Inspired by a magnified look of the calyx on a blueberry, which resembles a
crater (the remnant of the sepal—the base of the flower)

Star Map

> *And I will show wonders in the heavens and in the earth:*
> *blood, and fire, and pillars of smoke.*
> —Joel 2:30

It was after the Bible study down the road from
the observatory; its darkroom lab and archives.
The kerosene lamp flickered throughout the night
glinting off photographic glass plates, the silver
oxide betraying the smattering of stars outside
our galaxy. I almost missed it because of the glare
from the lamp as I scanned with magnifier in hand
—a humongous starburst, fireworks in the heavens
like no other imagined. It's as if the entire galaxy
exploded. Surrounding star clusters, more luminous
from the shattering of light of what was NGC-597,
and now the sky at night is black.

I've seen the equations, just didn't believe them
that a central black hole could explode like that—
sucking energy from another dimension; spilling it
into ours. Not just light and fast-moving particles
came out of that abyss. Before our sun turned into
darkness, and the moon, into blood, the desperate air
over mountains thundered with thousands of locust-
shaped ships—steeds of lion-maned aliens assaulting
our home. The Book of Joel spoke something of it,
and even though as an old man dreaming dreams,
like this, I didn't believe that either.

NGC-597 is a barred spiral galaxy, like the Milky Way, in the constellation
Sculptor

Voyager III

Delta Quadrant

For all mankind, I search for sentient life forms in the outer reaches of the galaxy / I search for the meaning of life / I hear myself dream / Cryogenic alarms sound, I blink / in the darkness, the whir of my breath is shallow / I am cold / pray perpetual winter is over / I feel alone; dead / circuits have been resurrected in an avalanche of dark matter / I shudder / A white glow blinds my sensors / Where am I? / I ask myself, but I don't answer / I see only the dull gray of my shadow / I am scared / *Master. Master! Please wake up!*

Breathe

I am dreaming in deep sleep—engulfed in a blue derivative of liquid perfluorohexane— extracting air dissolved in fluid, just as I did as a fetus until born into air.

My lungs drink in oxygen, steady and deep, my pulmonary pulses: sixteen breaths per minute. But I sense they are climbing, becoming erratic. Relax, I say to myself, this is a dream, right? And there's no pollen or mold, no smog or chemical pollutants to choke me, no asphyxiant, just pure air, clear and cold.

Eyes coming out of the blur, I focus on the navigation panel: still bound for Epsilon Eridani-3, a planet in the near distance, a mere five light-years to go. I am dreaming yet I am troubled, my breath fogging the glass of my protective pod. Wait! This is not a dream. I must have awakened from cryostasis ... much too early. There's no way to return to sleep, to submerge and fill my lungs with hope.

I'll drift into dreamless dreams, to lonely lullaby thrums inside the cage of my heart, and to the desperate breathing of the rocket engines rushing to get me home.

Ark II

Captain's Log, Earth-date December 25, 2121:

It's time
The jigsaw puzzle sky
Is backlit with the dawn
Of a new age; the fowl
Have already flown south
And all the beasts of the field
Have scattered; over the ridge
The ocean grows black

~~~

Prepare for launch
Electromagnetic storms
Approaching, atmospheric
Ablation, imminent

  Cargo is secure, Captain
  Winds southwesterly at three zero knots
  Temperature forty degrees Fahrenheit
  Temporal rift materializing at twelve-o-clock

Main engine start on my mark:
…three, two, one…
Engage rotating fields
<emergency alarms activate>

  The hull's creaking, Sir
  Approaching stress limits
  Throttling

Good
Monitor telemetry
Maintain trajectory
Accelerate to zero point four light-speed
~~~

Stabilizing
Magnetic coupling complete
Going superluminal

~~~

Target galaxy on sensors, Sir
Descending through Virgo cluster
Engaging dark matter decelerators

Well done
Planet on screen
Calculate orbital insertion
Prepare to land

~~~

Release the animals
Plant the flowers and herbs
And these two trees, the evergreens
    In the middle of the garden

Gliese 581g

The captain stares at the view screen.
Orbital insertion in two minutes.
On the approach path, the grip of gravity,
the lining up of holographic rectangles

ensures orbital insertion in two minutes,
it'll tremble the ship in the thin exosphere
inside holographic rectangles,
the rattle and shake of fuselage,

it trembles the ship. In the thin exosphere,
the vessel buffets and broncos as it slips,
it rattles and shakes the fuselage
as it enters the thicker atmosphere.

Though the vessel buffets and broncos as it slips
into alien air, its thermal shields hold
coming through the thicker atmosphere.
Touch down in thirty seconds.

Thermal shields holding through alien air,
thrusters in full reverse, ions blasting
through the thicker atmosphere
over the alien terrain. Methane rain

blasts thrusters. Full reverse, ions
pelt the fire-polished hull, vaporizing
methane rain over the alien terrain
on contact. Sparks scintillate spaceship,

pelt the fire-polished hull, vaporizing
outer layer of shell from leftover discharged static
on contact. Sparks scintillate spaceship
in the dielectric rain. Lights flicker

on the shell from discharged static leftover
from some grounded circuits
in the dielectric rain. Lights flicker
as the spaceship touches down

despite some grounded circuits.
But the Captain isn't smiling
as the spaceship touches down—
the metal creaks of the ship.

And the Captain isn't smiling.
It's not normal outside (weird trees)
and the metal is creaking all over the ship
that's dancing in the wind.

It's not normal outside (weird trees),
the captain stares through the view screen.
What's dancing in the wind?
What's that approaching? Its grip, its gravity.

The name Gliese 581 refers to the catalog number from the 1957 survey Gliese
Catalogue of Nearby Stars. This star is a red dwarf (spectral type M3V) 20.4
light-years from Earth in the constellation Libra. The exoplanet Gliese 581g is
a highly contested planet about twice Earth's mass in the middle of the habitable
zone.

On Kepler 452b

there is no gender
        inequality, though
                there once was:

men favored sports,
        wanted war; women
                prefered their children

to live. after the revolt
        civilization changed,
                a new polity evolved

for the collective good:
        no more gender bias,
                now all can squabble

with equal voice
        equal poetic rants
                and equal violence.

Kepler 452b was the first potentially habitable super Earth-sized exoplanet around a sun like ours, Earth's cousin so to speak (discovered July 2015). It is 1402 light-years away in the constellation Cygnus.

Waterworld

Twilight air, thin.
        Sun, setting hot red
                fills the sky scarlet,

yet the ocean, thick
with cool salty chalk,
ripples over my smooth

arms finning the wetness,
        my head barely above
                the ebb in the shallows.

I stare at the blackness
of space, unveiling
a million suns sifting

through cosmic dust. I ask,
        Can you see the center,
                that dazzle in Sagittarius?

My daughter squints through
the special glass. I wonder
if she thinks about midnight

worlds that canopy the sky
        with light. Those planets
                pinned on ends of the ecliptic,

shiny giant beads, one ringed
with crystals, the other reddish

brown with moons, so many moons.

I heard it on the news today.
            They found another one perhaps
                        like ours, a world that shook

its sun. *Can you see it?* I say,
That *star, near Omicron tauri!*
They think it has a waterworld

a hundred million miles
            from its sun,
                        its bright yellow sun.

Now hurry, we must dive deep.
The sun will soon shift from shadow
and the air is much too thin.

Author's Notes: This poem is based on Gliese 581c. The center of our galaxy is in Sagittarius. We cannot see it with our telescopes because there is a great deal of dust that scatters the visible light. However, longer wavelength light, like infrared (IR), will penetrate and allow one to see it.

Since the planet, Gliese 581c, orbits a red dwarf (Gliese 581) with a surface temperature of ~3800 K (our sun is a yellow dwarf with a surface temperature ~5800 K), the peak wavelength or "color" from such a sun (treated as a blackbody) will be in the infrared. Any being "evolved" on such a planet would have eyes most sensitive to IR.

It is suggested that this planet could be watery and/or rocky. I take it to be all water in this poem. I would have expected the atmosphere to be thick, with much carbon dioxide, but imagine a place where most of the gas is absorbed into the oceans and forms a very exotic coral reef world (but I don't develop that notion in the poem).

The air is thin (not much oxygen) and not much of anything to protect creatures on the surface from the very hostile environment from the x-ray bursts whenever the small red sun flares. The destruction of most of the atmosphere and deadly UV renders the planet unsafe when the sun is up. This is why I develop the mermaid-like sentient beings (which are telepathic) and have IR-sensitive eyes.

In the beginning, the reader might think that the story was developed on Earth, but clues that it is another world are present. This waterworld, which was discovered on Earth (April 2007) has potential to harbor life. I imagined beings in their waterworld discovering us.

With planetarium software, I was able to see that our sun would appear very bright to our eyes and even brighter to the IR eyes (which still see optical, but not much beyond the yellow, let alone green). Our bright yellow sun would appear to be in the constellation Taurus near a star called Omicron Tauri.

Keeper of the Stars

> *The sun has one kind of glory, while the moon and stars each have another*
> —1 Cor 15:41

> *There is not a single thing that does not glorify God with praise, but you do not understand their glorification.*
> —Quran 17:44

Stars pour into the spinning vortex
their sparkles swirl, blend.

It's no accident, the birth of stars,
their death. Even they have a soul.

I stand on the brink of a cosmic
precipice, and feel a holy wind

with my anemometer of heart
as stars whoosh past me. No star

is too big to avoid the maw
of its mouth, they too are swallowed.

I watch the stars, blown before final
flares blacken them. They are left

with a singular gift at the bottom
of their journey—a pot of gold!

Black abyss transforms to white—
blinding spire piercing into new heaven

I am left in the afterglow
with the stardust, their atoms

in the nebulous unknown
that will one day be reborn
                              as me.

About the Author

John C. Mannone achieved a PhD [all but the dissertation defense] in Electrical Engineering on expanded space charge theory in dielectric fluids (University of Tennessee, Knoxville, TN, 2002), an MS in Physics specializing in plasma physics (University of Tennessee, Knoxville, TN, 1988), an MS in Physical & Theoretical Chemistry specializing in photoelectron spectroscopy (Georgetown University, Washington, DC, 1978), and a BS in Chemistry (Loyola University, Baltimore, MD, 1970). His research interests are in astrophysical plasmas and electromagnetic theory.

As a research chemist for Martin Marietta Laboratories in Baltimore, he worked on life detection systems on the Viking missions as well as on accelerated aging of electro explosives used on the Voyager missions. He met Carl Sagan there, a visiting lecturer, before he became famous.

He served as a NASA/JPL Solar System Ambassador for Tennessee and editor of the *Journal of Radio Astronomy* for SARA.

He has a passion for the literary arts since 2004, and often fuses art with science.

Mannone has poems in *Windhover*, *North Dakota Quarterly*, *Poetry South*, *Baltimore Review*, and others. He won the Dwarf Stars Award (2020); was awarded an HWA Scholarship (2017), and a Jean Ritchie Fellowship (2017) in Appalachian literature. He served as the celebrity judge for the National Federation of State Poetry Societies (2018). His full-length collections are *Disabled Monsters* (Linnet's Wings Press, 2015), *Flux Lines* (Linnet's Wings Press, 2022), *Song of the Mountains* (Middle Creek Publishing, 2023, a Weatherford Award nominee), *Sacred Flute* (Iris Press, 2024, a semifinalist for the 2025 Tennessee Book Award), and *Dark Wind, Dark Water*, a novella-length horror fiction collection forthcoming from Mind's Eye Publishing (2025). He edits poetry for *Abyss & Apex* and *Silver Blade*. He's a retired professor

of physics teaching science, mathematics, and creative writing in East
Tennessee whenever he gets the opportunity.

http://jcmannone.wordpress.com
https://www.facebook.com/jcmannone/

SPACE
COWBOY